To my friend the camel—
you have my sympathy
—C.S.

Published in the United States by Random House Children's Books,
a division of Random House, Inc., New York, and simultaneously in Canada
by Random House of Canada Limited, Toronto.

www.randomhouse.com/kids

Library of Congress Cataloging-in-Publication Data
Carryl, Charles E. (Charles Edward), 1841–1920.
The camel's lament / by Charles Edward Carryl ; illustrated by Charles Santore. — 1st ed.
p. cm.
SUMMARY: A poem in which a camel compares his life with that of other animals of the world.
ISBN 0-375-81426-4 (trade) — ISBN 0-375-91426-9 (lib. bdg.)
1. Children's poetry, American. 2. Camels—Juvenile poetry.
[1. Camels—Poetry. 2. Animals—Poetry. 3. American poetry.] I. Santore, Charles, ill. II. Title.
PS1260.C65C36 2004 811'.4—dc22 2003022271

MANUFACTURED IN CHINA First Edition 10 9 8 7 6 5 4 3 2 1

THE CAMEL'S LAMENT

A poem by
Charles Edward Carryl

Illustrated by

Charles Santore

Random House 🏠 New York

Canary birds feed on sugar and seed,

parrots

have crackers to crunch;

and as for the
poodles,
they tell me the doodles

have chickens and cream for their lunch.

But there's never a question

about MY digestion—

anything does for me!

Cats, you're aware,

can repose in a chair,

chickens can roost upon rails;

puppies are able to sleep in a stable,

and oysters

can slumber in pails.

But no one supposes

a poor camel dozes—

anyplace does for me!

Lambs are enclosed

where it's never exposed,

coops are constructed for hens;

kittens

are treated to houses well heated,

and  pigs

are protected by pens.

But a camel comes handy

wherever it's sandy—

anywhere does for me!

People would laugh if you rode a giraffe

or mounted the back of an OX;

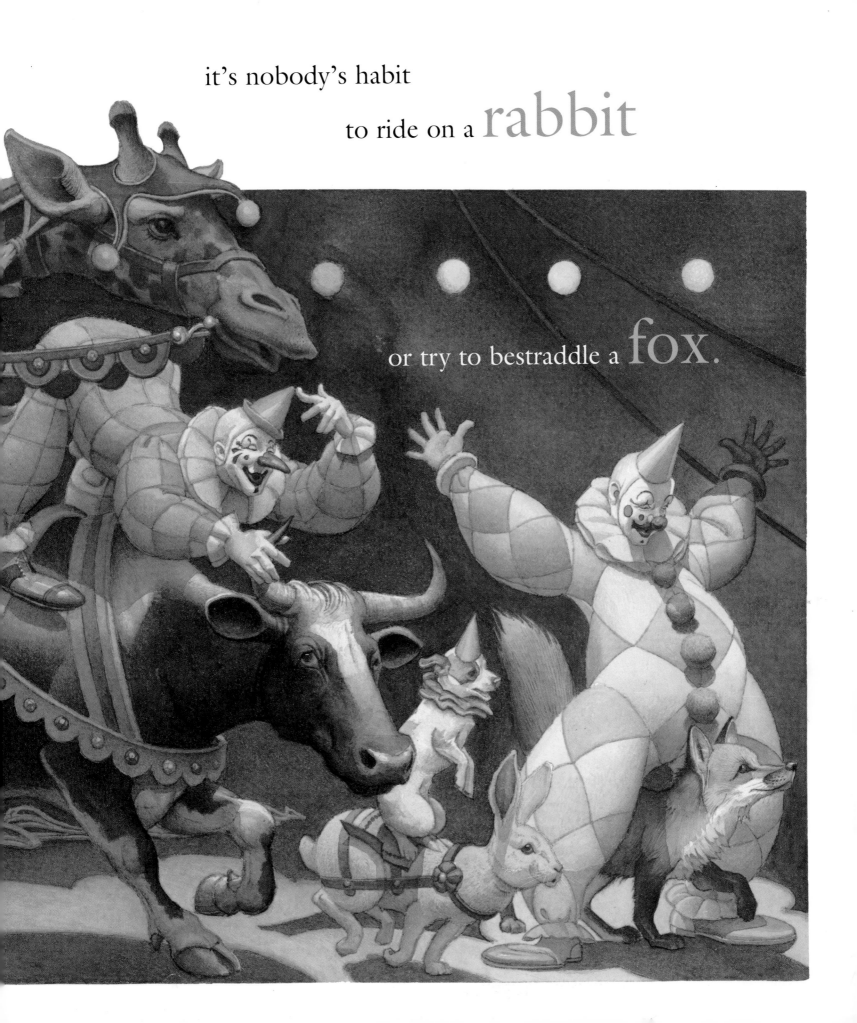

it's nobody's habit

to ride on a rabbit

or try to bestraddle a fox.

it's nobody's habit

But as for a camel, he's

ridden by families—

any load does for me!

A snake is as round as a hole in the ground, and **weasels** are wavy and sleek;

and no
alligator
could ever be straighter

than lizards
that live
in a creek.

But a camel's all lumpy

and bumpy and humpy—

ANY shape does for me!